A WOODLAND MYSTERY™

The Baseball Heroes

A WOODLAND MYSTERY
By Irene Schultz

To my sweet nephew, Jimmy Steinlauf,
who played baseball long ago

The Baseball Heroes
©1996 Wright Group Publishing, Inc.
©1996 Story by Irene Schultz
Cover and cameo illustrations by Taylor Bruce
Interior illustrations by Meredith Yasui
Map illustration by Alicia Kramer

Woodland Mysteries™
© Wright Group Publishing, Inc.

The Woodland Mysteries were created by the
Wright Group development team.

The Wright Group
19201 120th Avenue NE
Bothell, WA 98011

Printed in the United States of America

10 9 8 7 6 5 4 3

ISBN: 0-7802-7233-1

What family solves mysteries...has adventures all over the world...and loves oatmeal cookies?

It's the Woodlanders!

Sammy Westburg (10 years old)
His sister Kathy Westburg (13)
His brother Bill Westburg (14)
His best friend Dave Briggs (16)
His best grown-up friend Mrs. Tandy
And Mop, their little dog!

The children all lost their parents, but with Mrs. Tandy have made their own family.

Why are they called the Woodlanders? Because they live in a big house in the Bluff Lake woods. On Woodland Street!

Together they find fun, mystery, and adventure. What are they up to now?

Read on!

Meet the Woodlanders!

Sammy Westburg
Sammy is a ten-year-old wonder! He's big for his fifth-grade class, and big-mouthed, too. He has wild hair and makes awful spider faces. Even so, you can't help liking him.

Bill Westburg
Bill, fourteen, is friendly and strong, and only one inch taller than his brother Sammy. He loves Sammy, but pokes him to make him be quiet! He's in junior high.

Kathy Westburg
Kathy, thirteen, is small, shy, and smart. She wants to be a doctor some day! She loves to be with Dave, and her brothers kid her about it. She's in junior high, too.

Dave Briggs

Dave, sixteen, is tall and blond. He can't walk, so he uses a wheelchair and drives a special car. He likes coaching high-school sports, solving mysteries, and reading. And Kathy!

Mrs. Tandy

Sometimes the kids call her Mrs. T. She's Becky Tandy, their tall, thin, caring friend. She's always ready for a new adventure, and for making cookies!

Mop

Mop is the family's little tan dog. Sometimes they have to leave him behind with friends. But he'd much rather be running after Sammy.

Table of Contents

Chapter 1:
The Hopeless Nerd

It was Friday.

Next week was Kathy Westburg's week to be captain of the baseball team for her seventh-grade class.

And she HATED it!

Not that she hated baseball ... she hated the way they picked teams every Monday.

It was bad enough when SHE was nearly the last one picked.

But she felt even worse for a boy named Danny. He was ALWAYS the very last one picked.

In fact, last Monday both captains tried not to choose Danny at all.

Finally Mr. Coppelo, their classroom teacher, just put him on a team. The captain who got Danny grumbled about it all week long.

Kathy got up from the kitchen table. She saw that her brothers Sammy and Bill were almost ready to leave for school.

Dave Briggs, their sixteen-year-old friend, was reading in his wheelchair near the front door.

2

Then Mrs. Tandy walked in.

The five of them lived together as a family. They called themselves the Woodlanders.

Kathy felt she had to say something. She called, "Could you all come here for a second? I need some help."

She looked so worried that ten-year-old Sammy didn't even crack any jokes. They all came into the kitchen and gathered around her.

Dave said, "What's up, Kathy? What's wrong?"

Kathy said, "Well, I'm going to make half my class hate me.

"I'm going to pick Danny Musser first on my baseball team on Monday.

"Everyone else on the team will be mad at me.

"But I can't stand his being picked last ONE MORE TIME!

"And he's the worst player on EARTH!"

Fourteen-year-old Bill said, "Oh, I think I've seen him over at the junior high. Isn't he the one they call Mess?"

Kathy said, "Sometimes. But his real nickname is Mouse ... because everything makes him jump ... and he's always running around."

Bill said, "I do know who he is. His teeth stick out a little. He does look a little like a mouse."

Kathy said, "That's the one. He's really nice when you stop and talk to him.

4

But he's a real mess at school.

"And every time he's on a team, it loses. He gets all mixed up when he plays ball."

Bill smiled. He said, "Tell you what we could do.

"Go ahead and let him know you're going to choose him. But tell him this ... he will have to practice with us all weekend.

"You and Sammy and I are pretty good. And Dave helps coach his high-school team. And Mrs. Tandy was the star of the parent-teacher game. We can all help him, OK?"

Sammy said, "Watch out, world! When we are through with him, make way for SUPER-MOUSE!"

Everybody laughed.

Kathy said, "Thanks, guys. I'll talk to him today!"

At school, before class, Kathy looked for Mouse.

She found him near the front steps, on one knee.

He was trying to keep hold of four heavy books and his notebook.

He was tying his shoe at the same time.

The books slipped a little when he gave a hard pull on one lace.

The lace broke. His arms flew up. The books flew all around.

"DRAT!" he cried.

The notebook rings weren't snapped shut. Papers fell out.

They began to blow away.

Mouse began to run after them.

His shoe fell off.

He stepped down in a puddle in his sock.

"OH, SHOOT!" he muttered.

Kathy called, "STOP! JUST STAND STILL! I'll get your papers!"

She ran to pick them up. Most of them were only a little dirty.

She snapped them back into his notebook.

She said, "Let's go back to the steps and get your stuff together, Mouse."

Mouse said, "Thanks, Kathy. I'm a real mess."

Kathy picked his books up.

Mouse sat down on a step.

He had his broken lace in one hand and his shoe in the other.

He lifted his foot.

His wet sock hung on it like an old balloon.

Mouse leaned over to pull it off. This time a pair of glasses fell out of his shirt pocket.

He picked them up and jammed them back in.

Kathy said, "I didn't know you had glasses! You never wear them."

Mouse said, "I'm really near-sighted. I need them to see far away. But they keep slipping off."

Kathy said, "Is that why you have so much trouble with schoolwork, because you're near-sighted?"

Mouse looked at her strangely.

Then he said, "It's not because I'm near-sighted. If I tell you something, you won't laugh?   No, you probably won't, you've been so nice."

Kathy asked, "What is it?"

Mouse said, "You know when I leave class for forty-five minutes every day?

"Well, it isn't just for reading help. I'll tell you a secret."

Chapter 2:
A Bird, a Squirrel, and Mouse

Mouse looked around to see if anyone was near them.

He whispered, "When I go out for reading, it's for special help. I go to LD class."

Kathy said, "Oh, you mean the class for kids who have trouble learning? So, why do you need help?"

Mouse said, "When I look at a page I can't make sense out of it. I can't make the words stand still.

"And the letters change places. Is a word WAS or SAW? I can't tell.

"And letters seem backward or upside down. The letter 'p' could be a 'd' or 'b' or 'q'. And the letter 'u' looks like 'n' or 'c'."

Kathy said, "Well, you have to try to get some things un-mixed, this weekend. "You're first pick on my baseball team on Monday! But don't worry. My family's going to practice with you. If you'll let us!"

Mouse said, "Wow, Kathy. That's sure nice of you. But it's hopeless. Haven't you heard? I'm the hopeless nerd of

Bluff Lake Junior High."

At that moment something weird was happening. It was happening at the grade school, across the playground from the junior high.

Mrs. Chicca had Sammy's class out for a before-school nature walk.

As they came around the school corner they noticed a squirrel. It was limping.

A kid named Willie Bird ran after it.

Mrs. Chicca called, "Leave it alone, Willie! Stay away! It could claw you ... or bite you. It might have rabies!"

But Willie wouldn't stop chasing it.

The squirrel clawed its way up the school's brick wall.

Mrs. Chicca yelled, "Get back, Willie! It's scared! It might attack you!"

Willie shouted, "It's mine! I saw it first. I want it for a pet!"

Suddenly the squirrel fell from the

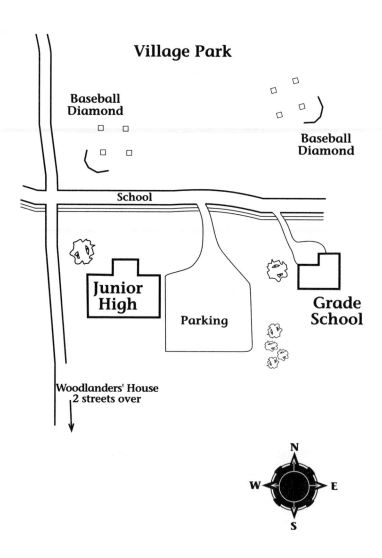

wall. It clawed the air wildly and landed on Willie's shoulder ... AND BIT HIM ON THE NECK!

Then it fell to the ground and limped away.

Mrs. Chicca shouted, "Now we've got to catch that animal!

"We have to test it for rabies!

"Someone run inside and get help!"

Sammy raced into the grade-school principal's office.

He shouted, "Mr. Dolan! COME QUICK! WE HAVE TO CATCH A SQUIR-REL THAT BIT WILLIE BIRD! BRING SOMETHING TO HIT IT WITH!"

Then he ran for Ms. Field, the grade school's P.E. teacher ... and Mr. Masters, the janitor. They all raced outside.

Sammy grabbed a broom.

Mr. Dolan held a yardstick in his hand.

Ms. Field waved a tennis racket.

15

Mr. Masters carried a big shovel.

Mrs. Chicca waved a branch.

The whole fifth grade ran along after them.

They chased that squirrel along the side of the school.

It ran through the bushes to the junior-high playground.

They followed it through the bushes. They ran across the playground shouting, "GET OUT OF THE WAY! SICK SQUIRREL!"

The junior-high kids spread out like pool balls on the opening shot.

The squirrel ran toward the steps where Mouse and Kathy were sitting.

Kathy jumped up the steps. "Get up here, Mouse!"

Mouse stood up. He tried to hold his books together.

Suddenly they flew out of his arms. THEY LANDED ON THE SQUIRREL!

16

A teacher ran up with a cardboard box.

Mr. Masters shoveled the limp squirrel into it.

Mrs. Chicca said, "Too bad it's hurt, but we had to catch it ... and just because you wouldn't listen, Willie."

Willie was crying and whining, "Now I've got rabies. I'll spit foam, and I'll get wild, and I'll bite people, and die!"

Mrs. Chicca said, "Calm down, Willie. You'll be perfectly all right. The only thing that has to die is this limp little squirrel.

"The public health department will have to test its brain for the rabies virus. They'll decide if you need rabies shots."

"SHOTS!" Willie bawled. "I hate shots!"

Sammy asked, "Would you rather get rabies, Willie?"

Willie sobbed, "If I did, you're the first one I'd bite, Sammy!"

Mrs. Chicca led Willie back to the grade school to call his parents.

Mr. Dolan turned to Mouse. He said, "Well done! That was a perfect shot. You have great aim!

"You'll be getting a Bluff Lake School Service award for this."

Then off he went, back to the grade school.

Kathy ran down the steps.

She said, "Mouse, that was great! You stopped that squirrel!"

But Mouse just picked up his books slowly.

He said, "It was all an accident, Kathy. Mr. Dolan was wrong. You know I don't have good aim.

"I wasn't even trying to hit the squirrel.

"My books slipped. They landed on that poor animal.

"It was all just a terrible accident.

"I would NEVER hurt a squirrel! Animals are my best friends. They never make fun of you.

"I wouldn't even kill a bug unless it tried to hurt me. I can't take any service award."

Mouse smiled sadly. "Maybe there's a

stupid award. I could win that, I guess."

Kathy said, "Cut it out, Mouse. You're not stupid! You just get ready for this weekend.

"We will be at your house tomorrow with baseballs and bats!"

Chapter 3:
Baseball Practice

It was 7:00 on Saturday morning.

The Woodlanders were up and dressed.

They made Sammy's favorite breakfast which was ...

scrambled eggs

orange slices

English muffins

milk

... and bananas.

Sammy mashed everyone's bananas with a fork. He poured milk and sugar into their bowls.

Bill said, "This is great, Sammy! It tastes like ice cream."

They all cleaned up while Kathy told them more about Mouse ...

about the glasses that fell off

how words moved on the page

how the letters changed around

... and how bad he felt about himself.

Sammy said, "Looks like Kathy's got a new boyfriend! She was on the steps with Mouse today at school. And she sure talks about him an awful lot."

Dave looked over at Kathy.

She blushed red and blurted out, "No, Dave is my ... "

Then she realized what she had started to say, and turned even redder.

She hurried out of the room and got out two baseball bats and two balls.

The others found their mitts ... and a piece of cardboard to use for a home plate.

Dave took a green plastic post from his closet ... and a bunch of rubber bands ... and some paper clips ... and a metal wire.

Mrs. Tandy said, "What are those for?"

Dave said, "I can't tell you. These are my secret weapons."

They took their little dog Mop on a long rope.

Off they went to Mouse's house.

His mother was at the door when they got there.

23

Mrs. Musser said, "Well, hello! I'm so glad you're going to help Danny at baseball! Come in! Have some sweet rolls!"

So they each ate one before Mouse came banging down the stairs.

Mrs. Musser invited them all to come back later for lunch.

Sammy said, "Sure! Playing baseball makes me hungry!"

Bill said, "Sammy, BREATHING makes you hungry!"

Then they walked off to the park.

The plan was that Kathy would pitch.

Mouse would practice batting.

Bill would catch.

Sammy would field to the left.

Mrs. Tandy would field to the right.

Dave would coach.

But the trouble began right away.

Mouse had his glasses on, but they slipped down every time he swung.

Kathy pitched about thirty pitches.

Mouse missed every one.

Then Kathy moved closer and pitched slower. But even then, if Mouse hit one, he fouled it over his head.

Once he fouled it ONTO his head!

By now Sammy was losing interest.

He was racing around with Mop.

Mrs. Tandy was wondering if they would ever get anywhere.

Then Dave said, "Mouse, let's start over. This time the ball will be standing still. And your glasses will stay on, too."

Mouse said, "OK by me! I'm sure not having any luck with the ball moving."

So Dave reached into the side pocket of his wheelchair. He took out the bunch of rubber bands and paper clips.

He put them together to make a long band for Mouse's glasses.

With the band around his head, Mouse's glasses stayed in place.

26

Then Dave held up the green plastic post. It had a spring near the top and a point at the other end. Dave stuck it in the ground.

He said, "Put the ball on top of it, and aim, and swing easy."

Kathy, Bill, and Mrs. Tandy played out in the field.

Sammy wandered away to pick wild daisies.

Mop took a nap under a bush.

Mouse practiced swinging at the ball.

Dave told him, "The trick is to get into the habit of looking at the ball every second. Never take your eyes off of it."

Half the time Mouse batted the plastic post instead of the ball.

Some of the time he swung way above the ball.

But SOMEtimes he would hit a good one.

In another hour Mouse was hitting the ball about a third of the time.

By noon he was hitting it most of the time.

He shouted, "I think I'm learning!"

Dave said, "You are! And after lunch you'll get even better. We can practice hitting the ball when it's moving!"

Mouse grinned happily.

He said, "I can't believe how great you guys are to spend your weekend on me. I wonder ... maybe you'd like to see what I've got in the backyard.

"You'll probably want to get right back to baseball after lunch, but ... well ... you might like it.

"I've got a zoo."

Bill said, "A zoo! We would love it! Lead us to it!"

Chapter 4:
A Lady Named Hank

First they went inside for lunch.

    Mrs. Musser had made ...

    roast chicken

    coleslaw with bits of apple in it

... and home-made chocolate chip cookies.

Mrs. Musser said, "Now don't think I make lunches like this every day! Usually it's peanut butter and jelly sandwiches. That's the lunch Danny and his brother like best."

Bill said, "I didn't know you had a brother, Mouse. Where is he?"

Mouse said, "Matt's at college already. He's the smart one.

"He's seventeen, and loves to study.

"He's so good, the college asked him to go there, FREE! I'll be lucky if I make it through junior high!"

Mrs. Musser said, "Don't say that, honey. You'll make it just fine."

Mouse said, "Mom has to read me most of my school books.

"It takes me too long to make sense out of them by myself.

"I'm a lot of extra work for her."

Mrs. Musser said, "You know you're worth it, Danny!"

Sammy said, "Don't keep putting yourself down, Mouse. After all, nobody's perfect!" He grinned. "Except me, of course."

Bill pretended to choke. "Perfectly weird, you mean!"

Dave said, "Mrs. Musser, this lunch was great!"

Mrs. Tandy said, "It was a treat! Now, what's this about a zoo?"

Mouse said, "You'll see. Follow me."

In the yard, shaded by bushes, stood boxes made of wood and wire.

Kathy said, "What's in those?"

Sammy yelled, "Yuck! There's a big, stringy bug in this one!"

Mouse called, "That's my praying mantis. See, she holds her hands together

31

like she's praying. Isn't she a beauty?"

Sammy said, "A BEAUTY! I'd call her an UGLY! She looks like she'd kill you for a nickel! She scares me."

Mouse laughed. "Well, stand back then. I'm setting her free now.

"I've kept her prisoner long enough. She has to go find dinner."

They watched the mantis walk out on stiff, long legs.

Dave said, "She looks like she's walking on stilts."

Sammy said, "I guess she's not that scary after all."

Mouse said, "Only if you were a male mantis. Then she'd munch you down for a meal after you two mated."

Mrs. Tandy said, "You don't mean it! She wouldn't!"

Dave said, "That's true, all right. I've read about it."

Mouse said, "I've SEEN it. She's not what you'd call loving."

Sammy said, "What's in the other cages?"

Mouse led them to a cage with a gray, furry possum inside it.

Kathy said, "Look at those sweet pink paws, and that cute nose!"

Bill said, "He's sleeping in the food bowl, the little pig! Where did you get him? And isn't it against the law to keep wild animals in cages?"

Mouse said, "Yes, usually. But we have a permit. So we get to take in hurt animals. We make them better and set them free!

"A dog caught this possum. And a neighbor brought him to me."

Kathy said, "How do you know THESE animals don't have rabies?"

Mouse said, "Well, you can't tell by looking. I wear long, thick gloves when I touch them, just in case."

Bill said, "What's in this big cage? Hey! It's five guinea pigs!"

Sammy ran over. He said, "Mouse, you lucky duck!

"Look at that black furry one.

"And the smooth brown one.

"And the black-and-white one with curly hair.

"And the long-haired white one.

"And here's the best one, this smooth white guy. He's as shiny as a peeled potato, and shaped just like one, too.

"I love him! How did you get them all? Were they sick, too?"

Mouse said, "No. I saved for weeks to buy that smooth brown one. I bought it a month ago. Its name is Hank.

"A week later I found a cage at our door, and a note.

"It said, 'I know you have one guinea pig. It must be sad being all alone. I'm moving, so I can't take care of these two. So I'm leaving them for you.'"

Dave said, "And where did the other two come from?"

Mouse said, "Some other mystery person left the black furry one and the long-haired white one in a box in our garage a few days later.

"I went from no guinea pigs to five guinea pigs in one month!"

Kathy said, "What in the world are you going to do with them all?"

Mouse said, "Sell them! I'm in the guinea pig business now.

"I'm going to keep the two females. They're both going to have babies pretty soon.

"And I'll keep the long-haired white male.

"I'm going to sell the others."

Sammy said, "I thought you were

keeping two female guinea pigs and only one male. How come you're keeping Hank?"

Mouse said, "Because I made a mistake. Hank turned out to be a lady. She's one of the ladies I'm keeping."

Kathy giggled. She said, "You could change her name to Hanky."

Sammy said, "If they're for sale, can I buy the smooth white one? I've already named him ... Potato."

Mouse said, "Nope. You can't buy him, Sammy. Because I'm giving him to you!

"I'll trade him for my baseball lessons!"

Chapter 5:
I'm Not That Rotten!

Sammy said, "I want to PAY for him. I wasn't hinting for you to give him to me!"

But Mouse said they HAD to take the

guinea pig, or he'd feel awful. So finally they did.

Then he showed them around some more.

He had a rabbit and a pair of lovebirds, one green, one blue.

He showed them the things he used to build cages, such as ...

wooden sticks, to frame the walls
a saw, to cut them to the right size
nails, to put them together
screen, to make walls
heavy-duty scissors, to cut screen
staple-nails, to fasten the screen
a hammer, to pound the nails in
hinges, for the cage doors
screws, to fasten the hinges
... and a screwdriver, to put in the screws.

Then they helped him feed the animals.

Suddenly a squirrel ran down from a tree. It darted toward Mouse.

Kathy exclaimed, "Watch out! Another squirrel attack!"

Mouse said, "Don't worry. It's Brush. He's my friend."

He sat down on the grass.

The squirrel jumped onto his shoulder.

Mouse took some sunflower seeds from his pocket. He fed them to Brush.

Mrs. Tandy said, "Well, look at that! How did he get so tame?"

Mouse said, "I found him in the grass when he was tiny. He fell from that nest." Mouse pointed to a big bunch of leaves, high up in an oak tree.

"I put him onto some soft rags in a box Mom gave me.

"I named him Brush because his tail looks like one.

"At first I fed him milk from a doll's bottle. Then I gave him bread and nuts.

"When he was full-grown and could hunt for food, I turned him loose.

"He still hangs out with me, though.

"Squirrels don't care if you're nerdy."

Bill said, "Come off it, Mouse. You're NOT a nerd! You're a great kid!"

Mouse said, "But don't you get it? At home, I'm fine. No problem. At school? I'm HOPELESS! I feel like I'll never get anywhere."

Kathy said, "Listen, Mouse. NOTHING

is hopeless. And if you ARE going to get some where, we need to go play ball!"

All Saturday afternoon the Woodlanders helped Mouse learn to bat.

Most of Sunday they worked on it, too.

He finally got pretty good!

Kathy smiled at Mouse. "Well, you're playing like everybody else on the team!"

He smiled back.

Then Bill said, "OK, Mouse. It's not over yet!"

Dave said, "Nope. We have about three hours left to practice. How's your fielding?"

Mouse said, "Fielding? It's terrible, that's how it is.

"Sometimes I'm afraid I'll get hit in he glasses, and I duck.

"If I do get my hands on the ball, I usually drop it.

43

"Or it hits me in the stomach.

"Or the head.

"Or my glasses fall off.

"Once the ball even got stuck in my glove. So I threw the whole glove to first base.

"The guy on first base caught my glove, but the ball fell out. That's how I am at fielding."

Mrs. Tandy said, "Well, at least you caught that ball. That's something."

Again Dave reached into his wheelchair pocket. He handed Mouse a wire mask.

He said, "First, put this wire thing on over your glasses.

"Now, when you go to catch the ball, don't try to stop it. Grab it and pull it toward your body.

"It's going to keep moving. So bring it in."

Mouse said, "I'll try."

So they worked on Mouse's catching. Next they worked on his throwing.

Kathy told him, "When you throw, your arm should end up aimed at your target."

Sammy said, "And use your whole body to throw, like this."

He threw himself forward ... and ended up flat on his face!

He said, "Well, not exactly your WHOLE body."

Bill said, "Keep looking at the person you're throwing to."

With his mind loaded with advice, Mouse began to practice.

When it got a little colder, they kept on practicing.

When they got hungry, they kept on practicing.

When Mrs. Tandy and Bill went off to make dinner, they kept on practicing.

When bugs began biting them, they kept on practicing.

Finally it got too dark to see.

They had to stop, but they felt good.

Even Mouse was happy.

He said, "Hey, I'm not that rotten anymore. Maybe you won't be sorry for picking me tomorrow, Kathy!"

Chapter 6:
Mouse on First

Monday finally came.

It was time for P.E.

Kathy and the other captain stood facing each other.

Ms. Day, the junior-high P.E. coach, said, "All right, class. Let's do this in a hurry.

"Kathy, you get first pick."

Kathy said, "I choose Mouse. Danny Musser."

Everyone looked at Kathy as if she were a space monster.

The other captain picked the best player in the class.

Then Kathy made her second choice.

The person she picked moaned.

Everyone HATED the idea of being on the same team as Mouse.

Some of the kids tried to hide when it was Kathy's turn to choose.

They KNEW they would lose!

Or at least, that's what they thought.

At last everyone was chosen.

They headed to the field next to the school.

Each captain wrote out a team batting order.

Kathy had her best player up first.

He hit a double and stood waiting at second base.

Kathy called out, "Mouse, you're up next!"

There were so many groans, the field sounded like a haunted house.

One boy said, "That's stupid. Mouse will strike out. Put Jeff up. Maybe he can hit a double. We could bring in at least one run to start us off right."

Kathy said, "No, Mouse has been

practicing. He's up next."

The boy said, "OK, it's your loss!"

Mouse heard him.

He turned to Kathy and said, "Don't put me up. I probably WILL strike out. I always do."

Kathy said, "Look, Mouse, it wouldn't matter if you DID strike out. We don't have any outs yet. But you WON'T strike out. You were hitting fine yesterday. You can do it today."

So Mouse stood up to home plate.

He put on his glasses and his mask.

He put on his batting helmet.

The other boy walked behind the chain-link backstop.

He called to a friend, "Here comes our first out!"

Mouse swung at the first pitch.

He tipped it foul.

The catcher almost got it, but just

missed ... so it wasn't an out.

Mouse said to Kathy, "See. I hit it foul."

Kathy said, "Everyone does that, Mouse."

The next pitch came in near Mouse's ankles.

"BALL ONE!" called the umpire.

The next was much too high.

"BALL TWO!"

The next was just right.

Mouse swung hard.

He missed it by a mile.

Now he had a strange look on his face.

Scared?

Ashamed?

Sad?

Angry?

Kathy couldn't tell.

She felt awful for him.

Just then Bill's class came pouring out the door.

Bill saw Mouse right away. From the look on Mouse's face, Bill guessed he was having a hard time.

He called, "Hey, Mouse! Remember how great you were doing yesterday ... how you were standing ... how you watched the ball?"

He pointed to Mouse's glasses. He winked and said, "And the glasses are magic! They'll get you to first! Wait and see!"

The pitcher threw again. Another ball.

Three balls and two strikes.

Then the pitcher threw again.

But Mouse never got a chance to find out whether he could have hit it.

Because the ball hit HIM! WHACK! Right on the leg!

Mouse grabbed hold of his leg.

The other kids crowded around him.

"Are you hurt?"

"Are you OK?"

The pitcher hurried over. "Boy, I'm sorry! Are you all right?"

Mouse said, "I'm OK. Don't worry."

Ms. Day looked at Mouse's leg.

She said, "It looks fine. But I bet it hurts!"

Mouse said, "It's OK. I'm pretty tough."

Then Ms. Day said, "That puts you on first base. You get hit by a pitch, you get the base free. That's the rule."

Mouse shot a smile at Bill.

He joked, "Bill, you were right! My glasses must be magic. I kept them on, and here I am on first."

Mouse didn't get up to bat again.

By the time seven other players on his team had been up, they had four runs and two outs.

When their best player was up again, he hit a pop fly.

Someone caught it and he was out.

Kathy whispered, "See, Mouse, you're not the only one who makes outs."

When P.E. was over, the score was four to two.

Kathy's team had won.

Ms. Day said, "Nice going, kids. Both your teams did a great job. Looks like Mr. Coppelo's here to take you back to class."

Mr. Coppelo walked up to the team

and said, "I've been watching you out my window.

"I was glad to see you play as well as you did.

"NOW I can tell you what I've been worrying about all week!"

Chapter 7:
The Dare

Mr. Coppelo talked to them right in
the hall.

He looked really upset.

He said, "You know the school in

Green Forest? Carmen Prep School?"

One of the boys said, "Sure, I even know a guy who goes there.

"He's always bragging that their school is better than ours.

"And he brags about their uniforms ... and everything else."

Mr. Coppelo went on. "Well, their seventh-grade teacher is a man named Stanford Twerk.

"He's DARED us to play his seventh-grade team two weeks from today.

"He says his students are the best in everything, including baseball.

"He says we are a bunch of cream puffs, and don't stand a chance to win.

"He says I would be afraid to let my students play his students.

"They call themselves the Carmen Cannons."

The whole class began to talk all

at once.

"That guy's ASKING for it!"

"We could beat them! We could make a team out of our best players!"

Mr. Coppelo said, "Can't. He dared ALL of our class to play ALL of his.

"And they've been practicing for two weeks already, every day, after school. Another teacher told me."

One of the kids said, "Then we could NEVER beat them!"

But Mouse said, "Well, why couldn't we?

We have two weeks to get ready. We could work TWICE as hard as they do!

"Kathy's family helped me in just one weekend.

"Maybe Mr. Coppelo would coach us before and after school. AND weekends.

"Maybe we COULD play as well as they do. Better!"

But Mr. Coppelo said, "Sorry, kids.

"I have to be out of town the next two weekends.

"I'm going to my brother's wedding, and a state teachers' meeting."

He looked down-in-the-mouth as he walked with them back to their room.

Standing inside the door was a stranger.

Mr. Coppelo said, "Oh, hello, Nick! Class, this is Nick Landers. He's here to talk to you ... and some visitors ... for Career Education.

"Mr. Dolan from the grade school

asked me to take a fifth-grade class in with us for this hour.

"Their speaker for Career Ed couldn't come today. I told him they wouldn't be any trouble.

"It's your brother's class, Kathy.

"Sammy ... isn't that your brother's name? Well, he will be here.

"Now make room for a little fifth grader, everyone."

Kathy laughed and said, "NO TROUBLE? LITTLE fifth grader?

"You've never met my brother, Mr. Coppelo! You better get an armchair and a bear trainer in for Sammy!"

Just then the fifth graders came trotting in. When Mr. Coppelo saw Sammy, he turned his own big chair over to him.

Mr. Landers smiled and called to Sammy, "Hi there, Sammy."

Sammy said, "Oh ... wait ... I know you. I met you when Mrs. Tandy was at the hospital for an X ray."

Mr. Landers said, "I remember you and your brother. And now I remember your sister Kathy over there, and a young man in a wheelchair ... Dave, I think.

"You were all in the waiting room.

"How could I ever forget you! You asked me two thousand questions about Mrs. Tandy and her X ray.

"I thought you'd never let me take her to the X-ray room."

Sammy said, "Well, I sort of take care of her. She counts on me."

Kathy said, "I remember you, too, Mr. Landers. You do bone scans ... and CAT scans, right?"

Mr. Landers said, "Yes, I can do them all.

"But I had many other jobs before I came to work at the hospital.

"I'm here to tell you to aim high. When you finally see what you want, go for it. It may take years of work to get there.

"You may have to set new goals.

"But try for it!"

Mouse grinned and said, "Does that go for playing baseball, too?"

Mr. Landers said, "Sure. You having baseball troubles?"

Mouse said, "Our whole class is."

A girl sitting next to Mouse said, "We might play a team that's been practicing for weeks to beat us."

Mr. Coppelo said, "Come on, class. Let's quiet down. Nick didn't come here to hear about our baseball troubles."

But Mr. Landers said, "As a matter of fact, I'm very interested. I love baseball. I used to coach Little League back in my home town."

So in one minute they told him about Carmen Prep School, and being called cream puffs, and having only two weeks to shape up.

Mr. Landers said, "Well, first, on with Career Education.

"I want to tell you about my first job, when I was ten.

"Then I'll tell you about what I do today.

"And then let's think about your base-ball problem.

"I might have an idea or two to help!"

Chapter 8:
My First Job

Mr. Landers said, "So let's see ... my first job. I got it by accident.

"One day my friend asked if I could deliver his newspapers for a month while he was away.

"I said sure!

"I thought it would be a snap and I'd be rich.

"But you'll never guess what it was really like!"

Suddenly Sammy's hand shot up. He waved it wildly and jumped up.

He called out, "I can guess. I bet everything was horrible at first!"

Kathy was afraid Sammy would get in trouble for butting in.

But instead of being mad, Mr. Landers laughed out loud. He said, "That's right. How did you know?"

Sammy said, "Because my brother Bill and I used to have a paper route. The first few months it was rotten!"

Mr. Landers said, "Then you tell the class about it, and save my voice. Come right up here to the front."

Sammy trotted up.

He said, "Well, first we had to roll the newspapers.

"Then if it was rainy we had to put them into plastic bags.

"The papers HAVE to stay dry. YOU'RE what gets wet!

"Once we forgot our rain coats. We got as wet as dish rags!

"Our mom made us un-dress on the

porch before she let us in!"

A girl sitting in the front row giggled.

Sammy made his poison-spider face at her and went on.

He said, "When it wasn't raining, we just put rubber bands around the papers, and threw them, like this."

He picked up a newspaper from Mr. Coppelo's desk. He wrapped a rubber band around it. He threw it to the back of the room.

The paper hit a boy in the head.

Sammy said, "Oops, I'm SORRY!"

The boy and the rest of the room just laughed.

He went on. "It was really hard to find some of the houses.

"And sometimes I missed the porch when I threw. I had to go pick up the paper.

"Once I got into so much mud, my

feet looked size eighteen, like the abominable snowman's."

Mr. Landers and Mr. Coppelo were smiling. So was the rest of the class.

Sammy said, "Once I threw a paper onto a porch roof.

"The guy got so mad, he swelled up like a bullfrog. I was afraid he'd explode!

"Boy, was I careful after that!"

Mr. Landers laughed. "I bet you were, Sammy. What else happened?"

Sammy said, "Well, once a giant dog flew out and tried to bite us. Like this!"

Sammy raced across the front of the room. He made his mad-dog face. He barked wildly.

Mr. Coppelo said, "This is the best show I've seen in weeks!"

Sammy said, "Well, it really scared me!

"Once Bill and I woke up really late.

"We threw on our clothes over our pajamas and went to work.

"And then we went straight to school that way. I didn't know it until I got there, but my pajama leg was hanging out of my pants leg!

"And the day the truck dropped off the first SUNDAY papers, we nearly DIED! They weighed about a thousand pounds each!"

Sammy picked up a scrap of paper. He pretended to be falling to the floor under its weight.

"And once we were both sick. Mom took the papers around in the car.

"And once the bottom of my jeans got caught in my bike chain.

"My bike wouldn't move one inch."

Kathy said, "I remember that. Bill had to cut a chunk out of your pants to get you home."

Sammy went on. "Then in winter the snowstorms hit. We couldn't ride our bikes. We had to pull the papers around on sleds.

"But now I'll tell you the hard part."

A girl said, "I thought you WERE telling us the hard part."

Sammy said, "No, the hard part was, we had to collect money."

The girl asked, "What's so hard about that?"

Sammy said, "Lots of times people were out. Or they didn't have money with them. We had to go back over and over to get it."

Mr. Coppelo said, "Now I want to ask you a question, Sammy. Why did you keep working at such a hard job? Why didn't you quit?"

Chapter 9:
What If ... ?

Sammy said, "Well, I liked having money.

"I had to save some of it for college. But I could use some to buy stuff. I didn't have to ask my folks for money all the time. I even bought my own bike."

Mr. Landers said, "Is that the only reason you stuck with your job?"

Sammy said, "Well, no. It may sound stupid, but I liked working. I got to be really good at it, and people counted on me. And boy, did I get the presents at the holidays!"

Mr. Landers said, "Well, kids, I had pretty much the same things happen when I handed out papers.

"As I got older I kept looking for better jobs. A dog walker. A waiter. Sales. But none of my jobs was ever as hard as delivering papers!"

Kathy said, "Well, what about now?"

Mr. Landers said, "I decided what I really wanted to be was an X-ray expert.

"I saved every cent I could.

"I went to college when I was twenty-eight ... ten years older than almost everyone else there.

"I discovered you can work to be whatever you want to be.

"Now, do you have any questions?"

This time Mouse's hand shot up.

He said, "I have a question."

For a second his face looked twisted up, like the face of someone who's going to cry.

But instead of crying, he gave a little laugh ... that didn't sound happy at all.

He said, "What good would all your hard work be if you saved all your money and were like me?

"What if you had trouble learning?

77

"What if you could never learn to read and spell?

"What if you always felt dumb?"

For a minute everyone was so surprised, no one spoke.

Then Mr. Landers said, "Young man, what's your name?"

He said, "Mouse. I mean Danny Musser."

Mr. Landers said, "Well, Danny, you just asked a very important question.

"But I think what you SHOULD ask is, 'What if you haven't learned to read and spell YET?'

"What if you have a learning disability?" He said the word like this: dis-uh-BILL-it-ee.

He went on. "Are you in an LD class? A learning disability class?"

Mouse nodded.

Mr. Landers said, "Believe me, I know how hard it can be. But you have to keep trying.

"And anyway, what makes you think that not being good at schoolwork is the same as not being smart?"

Mouse said, "Well, of course it is."

Mr. Landers said, "Well, of course it ISN'T!"

Chapter 10:
Mr. Landers to the Rescue

Mr. Landers said, "Danny, I won't say how, but I know a lot about having trouble in school.

"And I happen to be an expert on

learning disabilities.

"So stop feeling sorry for yourself, and listen to what I have to tell you.

"Have you ever heard of Albert Einstein?"

Mouse said, "Wasn't he that math genius?"

Mr. Landers said, "You're exactly right. Did you know that he was slow at learning to talk?

"And he was absent-minded, always staring off into space.

"One teacher told his parents he couldn't learn. She told Albert it would be best if he left school.

"But he loved math. And he didn't quit learning. And he came up with the idea that led to splitting the atom.

"Some dummy, huh?"

Mr. Coppelo broke in. "Say, Danny! In fifth grade did you study about

Thomas Edison?"

Mouse said, "Sure. He was the one who invented light bulbs."

Mr. Coppelo said, "Did you know he was terrible at school?

"He couldn't remember things he was supposed to. His spelling was awful.

"And he kept asking all sorts of strange questions. His teachers couldn't stand him.

"At home he kept messing around with a chemistry set. And blowing things up by accident.

"But he sold newspapers on a train when he was twelve.

"He began to learn about electricity from using a railroad telegraph.

"He never DID learn how to spell.

"But he invented electric lights.

"Some dummy, huh?"

Mr. Coppelo went on. "Mouse, I want

you to think about all the things you do WELL. There are a lot of different ways to be smart. And a lot more important things than reading!"

Sammy said, "MR. COPPELO! I can't believe you said that!

"You're a TEACHER!

"What if the principal hears you?"

Mr. Coppelo laughed.

He said, "Listen, Sammy. Mouse's main job is to keep trying to read better, no matter how hard it seems.

"But more important, he has to know he's a fine person ... no matter what."

Then Mr. Landers said, "Well, I'm taking on a new main job.

"If you kids will meet with me every day before and after school, and on the next two weekends ... then I'll coach you at baseball.

"And will we give those Carmen kids

a run for their money!"

Everybody stood up and cheered.

Sammy was the loudest.

They were still cheering when the bell rang.

The classroom emptied out.

Mr. Coppelo turned to Mr. Landers. He asked, "Do you really think they can do it?"

Mr. Landers answered, "Well, it won't be easy. At all. But I think they stand a pretty good chance."

Mr. Coppelo was ready to go outside, but he had one more question.

He asked, "By the way ... what made you such an expert on learning disabilities?"

Mr. Landers' face twisted a little. Then he gave a little laugh. "That's a story I might tell you someday.

"For now, you get the kids started practicing, and I'll be back at 4:30!"

Chapter 11:
The Cheerleader Leader

After Career Ed was over, Sammy and Kathy waited outside Bill's classroom door.

The minute he came out, they both began talking to him at the same time.

Sammy said, "Let ME tell him, Kathy! I never get a chance to talk!"

Kathy laughed and said, "Sammy, you were talking half of last period! Besides, whose class is it that's going to play against Carmen Prep?"

Sammy said, "See that? You've told him the whole thing already! Now let me say just one sentence!"

Here was his sentence:

"The game's going to be two weeks from today ... and that X-ray man we met was here for Career Ed ... and I told him all about when we had our old paper route and he's going to coach ...

"... and everyone in Kathy's class is on the team ... and the Carmen teacher is Mr. Twerk ... and he says our players are just cream puffs ...

" ... and our team is practicing every day, even weekends ... and I'm going to help them ... and will you and Dave and Mrs. Tandy help, too?"

He came up for air. Then he said, "There now, Kathy, it's your turn to tell the rest."

Kathy laughed. "What rest? Well, I have to go and practice. There's Mr. Coppelo now!"

Bill called, "I'll go home and get

89

Mrs. T. and Dave. I'll be right back."

Kathy's class started right in.

They took turns batting and fielding.

They practiced pitching.

Bill came back with Dave and Mrs. Tandy, and they helped coach.

Mr. Landers got back to the school at 4:30.

He gave directions to each player up at bat.

"Hold that bat down further.

"Stand closer to the plate.

"Turn your body a little more toward me.

"Follow through on your swing. Let the bat follow the ball.

"Watch that ball every minute.

"Start your swing sooner.

"Choose your strikes carefully. Don't swing at every ball.

"Don't throw your bat like that. You

could hurt someone. You'd be thrown out of the game, and we need you!"

About forty kids from fourth and fifth grades had come back to school to watch the practice.

Even mean Willie Bird came.

They began cheering for every good play.

Suddenly Sammy got an idea.

He said, "Hey, let's be regular cheerleaders!

"And I get to be cheerleader leader, because I thought of it."

The others agreed ... except Willie Bird.

He got a sour look on his face.

He whispered, "I could do it better than that big slob!"

But all the kids were watching Sammy.

One of the girls said, "Hey, Sammy, let's make up some cheers."

A boy said, "What rhymes with Carmen?"

Another boy said, "How about this?
"Poor old CARmen
Won't go very FAR, men!"
Sammy said, "That's GREAT!"
Willie said, "It's STUPID!"

But Sammy turned to a boy with a notebook. He said, "Rob, will you write all these down?"

A girl named Maria said, "How about aLARmin'? You know, like alarming. It almost rhymes if you leave off the G."

Another girl said, "How about CHARmin', then?"

Sammy said, "Hey, how about STAR men? How's this?

"STAR women, STAR men,
OUR team is CHARmin'
Let's alARM old CARmen
They WON'T get very FAR, then!"

Willie said, "That really stinks!"

Maria said, "Why don't you make up a better one then, Willie, if you don't like ours?"

One of the others said, "It's a good cheer. Write that one down, Rob."

Then a girl said, "How about this?

"POOR old CARmen
PACK 'em in a JAR, then
SHOOT 'em to a star, and
THAT'S the end of CARmen!"

Willie said, "That stinks!"

93

Sammy said, "No, it's GREAT! Hey, we have to copy these cheers from Rob. Here, I've got more paper in my notebook."

Willie started copying the cheers. He said, "I hate doing this. This stinks!"

Then they began to practice cheering.

One of the kids did a fancy little step at the end of one cheer.

Willie said, "That stinks!"

But at last Maria said, "Hey, do you realize these cheers are mostly against THEM?

"We hardly have any cheers about OUR team being great.

"And our team doesn't even have a name!"

Sammy said, "Now that REALLY stinks!"

So he called over to the seventh graders, "Is it all right if we think of a team name for you?"

94

Someone answered, "Sure, if we like what you come up with."

So they started listing names.

"The Bluff Lakers? Too boring."

"The Lakers? Taken."

"The Stars? Taken."

"The Supermen? Not fair to girls."

Rob said, "It should be a name that sounds strong, like the Wolves. No, nothing rhymes with wolves. It should be something that we can make rhymes with. The Bats?"

Sammy said, "If we call ourselves the bats, they'll say we are batty."

Then Willie piped up, "Your names stink! I know the perfect name."

In a scary, shaky voice he howled, "The Ghosts!"

Sammy said, "I wish I could say that stinks. But it doesn't. It's the perfect name!"

Chapter 12:
Play Ball!

Before they knew it, two weeks had passed.

The Ghosts had practiced hard.

Sammy's group of cheerleaders had

their cheers down pat.

"We DON'T want to BOAST
when we smear them on TOAST!
SOFT-AS-JELLY CARMEN!
FEED 'em to a GHOST!"

"ASK any GHOST!
WE are the MOST!
WE are the BEST from
COAST to COAST!"

"With a G and an H and an O-S-T,
GHOSTS will beat CARmen
One-two-THREE!"

The park next to the school was packed with people.

Bill looked around and said, "Wow! Look at this park. It's a beehive."

Every seventh grader's mother or father who didn't have to work was there.

Every younger sister and brother was wandering around.

Many Bluff Lake teachers sat in the bleachers.

Mrs. Tandy and some mothers and grandmothers and one aunt walked up to the team. They had brought a surprise.

They had dyed a T-shirt black for each player.

They had sewn a white ghost onto the front of each shirt.

Dave handed the shirts out.

Mouse and Kathy put their shirts right on.

They felt wonderful, for a minute.

Then a pale blue bus pulled up.

In fancy letters on the side were the words CARMEN SCHOOL.

Out of the bus poured twenty-one seventh graders, dressed in REAL BASE-BALL UNIFORMS ...

shiny light blue pants with red stripes
light blue shirts with red neck bands
red and blue striped socks

... and caps that said CARMEN CANNONS.

Kathy and Mouse took one look at them.

They looked back down at their own faded jeans and old P.E. shoes.

But good old Sammy finally said, "Who cares? THEY look like cream puffs!"

Next, twenty cheerleaders got out of the bus.

Both boy and girl cheerleaders wore shiny blue uniforms.

They waved silver and red pom-poms that sparkled in the sunlight.

They had megaphones to shout with.

Willie said, "Boy! Look at them!

"And look at us cheerleaders!

"We stink! All except me. I've got on my new white jeans."

Then about twenty teachers poured off the bus.

One of them, in a baseball uniform, was Stanford Twerk.

101

Mrs. Tandy whispered to Bill, "He smiles a little like the cat in *Alice in Wonderland*. You know, the smile stays even after the cat disappears."

Bill said, "Sure, he's probably thinking of us as a mouse dinner."

He looked over at Mouse, who looked really scared, and about as white as his Ghost T-shirt. "But I hope not a Mouse dinner."

The Carmen teachers walked right past the Bluff Lake bunch and sat down by themselves.

Mrs. Tandy whispered to Dave, "I love these FRIENDLY little inter-school games!"

But just then Mr. Landers boomed out, "PLAY BALL!"

The game was about to begin.

Chapter 13:
Hip Hip Hooray!

The Carmen cheerleaders started to cheer:
"CARmen CANNONS, 'RAY hooRAY!
THEY can BEAT you ANY day!
BLUE and RED will GET AHEAD!

RED and BLUE will WIN from YOU! HOORAY!"

They waved their pom-poms and did fancy dance steps.

Then they gave the same cheer again. Then they gave it again. And again. And again.

Sammy said, "Hey! That's all they have, that one cheer! Listen to this. I just made up an answer to it.

"BLUE and RED can't get AHEAD

TRY your MOST, can't hurt a GHOST!"

Every time they cheered, Sammy's cheerleaders shouted back his new cheer. Then they gave one of their other cheers. And were they LOUD!

The Ghosts played great ball.

By the second half of the ninth inning, the score was close ... twelve to thirteen ... but in favor of the Carmen Cannons.

The Ghosts had a runner on third.
Mouse was up to bat.

After two weeks, he was in good shape.

He could hit a single, maybe, and tie up the game.

He stepped up to the plate.

He placed his feet carefully.

He lifted his bat.

He looked all around to make sure no one was in the way.

Suddenly Mouse's eyes rested on a little girl. She was standing behind the backstop near Sammy.

She had a vine in her hand.

105

She was lifting the berries on it toward her open mouth.

Suddenly Mouse threw down his bat.

He shouted, "Sammy! STOP THAT KID! DON'T LET HER EAT THAT!"

The pitcher threw the ball, but Mouse was long gone.

He was running around the backstop.

Sammy grabbed the girl and held her arms behind her.

Mouse grabbed the vine out of her hands.

She started screaming.

Dave called out, "Hey! Those are deadly nightshade berries! They would have killed her!"

The child's mother rushed over. She said, "You boys are wonderful. I can never thank you enough. You saved my daughter's life. I know ... my husband can go for a treat ... a treat for everyone here!"

Mr. Twerk walked up to where Mr. Coppelo was sitting. He sneered, "Too bad, Coppelo. I just felt a few drops of rain on my face.

"The game is off, and my team is ahead.

"Your mixed-up batter, there, just lost the game for you. Maybe he should have stayed at home plate."

Mr. Coppelo said, "Calling off the game is fine with us, Mr. Twerk. But that batter is far from mixed up.

"He's a hero, and so is Sammy, there.

"And we didn't lose. Did you forget? In case of rain, the score goes back to the last full inning. We were tied, then, twelve to twelve."

Mr. Coppelo turned and walked away.

The rain began to pound down. Everyone dashed into the school.

The little girl's father came back with two hundred ice-cream bars and four hundred oatmeal cookies.

They all hurried down to the lunchroom.

The Woodlanders sat at a table with Mr. Landers, Mr. Coppelo, Mouse, and Mrs. Musser.

Mr. Landers said, "I want to tell everyone at this table something, but will you keep it a secret?"

They nodded yes.

Mr. Landers said, "Danny, when I heard you talking in class that day two weeks ago, do you know what I heard? I heard myself at your age.

"You see, I never learned to read well in school, either.

"I have a learning disability myself.

"But I finally discovered I could work with computers. I could learn how to take X rays. I discovered what I was good at.

"You're bright. You can discover what you're good at, too."

Mouse thought for a while.

He said, "Well, I did think about some things I can do, like Mr. Coppelo said.

"I talk well, and I can run fast.

"I can take care of bugs and animals.

"I learn all I can about plants.

"I'm strong, and I can play baseball.

"I don't give up so easily anymore.

"And ... maybe I'm not a hopeless nerd after all.

"I guess I'm not such a mouse."

Bill said, "No, you're more like a

moose, strong and fast."

Sammy said, "Moose? MOOSE? That's a great new name for Mouse! In fact, I was going to say that! You stole my idea, Bill."

He poked Bill on the leg.

At that Mr. Coppelo did something against the school rules ... and he was a teacher!

He climbed up and STOOD on the lunch table.

The kids almost choked.

He shouted, "It's time to give three cheers for the heroes of the baseball game ... Sammy Westburg and MOOSE Musser!"

The whole crowd roared,

"SAMMY and MOOSE, hip hip hooRAY! SAMMY and MOOSE, hip hip hooRAY! SAMMY and MOOSE, hip hip hooRAY!"

Then the Cannons and the Ghosts finally sat together, talking and laughing and munching cookies.